Poppy's Best Paper

◔◔ Charlesbridge

Poppy loved books. "I might be a writer when I grow up," she told her best friend, Lavender.

"I thought you wanted to be a brain surgeon like me," said Lavender.

"I'm still deciding," said Poppy.

"Me, too," said Lavender.

Ding! Mrs. Rose rang the Ringy Thing.

"Class, today's writing topic is
What I Want to Be When I Grow Up.
Tomorrow I will choose someone's paper
to read aloud. Remember to do your
personal best!"

"Oh boy!" shouted Poppy. "I'm going to be
a verrryyy famous writer when I grow up."

"I'm going to win prizes and talk at schools."

And that's how I became this verrryyy famous writer...

"I might write fifty books or a hundred . . ."

100 LITTLE RABBITS
Another great book by Poppy

I'm your number one fan!

Poppy's signing session

Mrs. Rose smiled. "Poppy, I like your enthusiasm, but please save it for your paper."

At the bus stop Poppy asked Lavender,
"Want to come over and write?"

"Sounds fun!" said Lavender.
"But I write better by myself."
"Oh," said Poppy. "Okay."

TOOT!

TOOT!

TOOT!

TOOT!

SCHOOL BUS

At home Poppy found Mr. Fuzz Dog.

She found her favorite notebook.

She sharpened her pencils.

She settled onto her bed. She wrote:

When I grow up
I want to be a writer.

She read her sentence. She wrote:

I am good at writing.
My dog likes the stories I write.

She phoned Lavender. "I have just written the best paper!
I know Mrs. Rose will pick it!"
"Already?" said Lavender.
Poppy read it aloud.

bip bip bip

"Don't you think it's good?"
asked Poppy.

Lavender was silent.
Then she said,
"I think you need to
write some more."

Poppy was silent.

"I'm still working on mine, too,"
said Lavender. "See you tomorrow."

Poppy read her paper again.
She added:

I will be famous.
The End.

Poppy hugged herself.
It was pretty much perfect.

The next day Mrs. Rose rang the Ringy Thing. "Class, your future goals are fascinating! Here's a paper that really stood out."

Poppy smoothed her fur. She licked her paw and polished her ear. She smiled modestly.

Mrs. Rose read, "Why I Want to Be a Brain Surgeon,
by Lavender Bloom."
Lavender! Poppy gave her a huffy face.

Poppy whispered to Petunia, "Can you believe it?
She doesn't even want to be a writer
when she grows up!"

shhhh!

Mrs. Rose announced, "Class, your next topic
will be If I Had One Wish."

At the bus stop Lavender asked,
"Are you mad at me?"

"No." Poppy fibbed.

At home Poppy told Mr. Fuzz Dog, "I am going to write the BEST paper ever!"
She wrote: IF I Had One Wish

She took a break.

She wrote some more:
I would wish to have my paper read out loud to the class.

She took another break.

Treasure ahead!

Then maybe my paper would be read to the whole school.

She phoned Lavender. "Whew, I've been writing for hours."

"Me, too," said Lavender. "Do you want to read me your paper?"

"Are you going to copy it?" asked Poppy.

"Of course not!" said Lavender.

"No, thanks," said Poppy. "I write better by myself."

Time for a break.

Time for dinner.

...and then Mr. Fuzz Dog was our lookout...

Time for bed.

la la la

ZZZZ

Time for school.

Wait! I haven't finished my paper!

On the bus Poppy scribbled an ending:

Then the principal would give me
a Good Writing Award. The End.

She gave a happy sigh.

She just knew her paper would be picked.

After recess Mrs. Rose
rang the Ringy Thing.

"Class, you have some wonderful wishes. This one is quite inspiring," she said.

Poppy smoothed her fur. She licked her paw and polished her ear.

She smiled modestly.

"My Wish for World Peace, by Lavender Bloom," read Mrs. Rose.

Poppy slumped.

She gave Lavender a mean look.

"You didn't even wish to win," she hissed at Lavender.

Mrs. Rose said quietly, "Poppy, please pay attention."

"Lavender doesn't even WANT to be a writer when she grows up!" complained Poppy.

"Poppy, I know you have lots to say, but please don't be rude."

"Poppy, it's time for a break
in the Chill-Out Chair.
Now, class, your next topic will
be How to Do Something."

At the bus stop Lavender wrote in her notebook
instead of talking to Poppy as usual. Poppy wondered
what Lavender was writing.

She wondered verrryyy hard.

"Poppy, are you copying Lavender?"
asked Petunia.

"Of course not!" said Poppy.

At home Poppy found her notebook.
She sharpened her pencils.
She wrote a sentence.

She played with Mr. Fuzz Dog.

She wrote another sentence.

She read what she had written.

She threw her notebook across the room.

"Go away,
Scraggle Tail!"
she shouted.

"Poppy! Do not call
your brother names!"
her mother said.

At dinner Poppy stirred her food into mush.
She spilled her milk and was not sorry.

"Go to your room!"
her father said.

Poppy stomped to her room and · · ·

Stomp
Stomp
Stomp
Stomp
Stomp

slammed the door.

BANG!

She cried to Mr. Fuzz Dog.

Young lady! You had better be doing your homework!

Poppy took out her notebook.

She sharpened her pencil.   She broke it in half.   She cried.

She sharpened another pencil.
Then . . . she had an idea.

She wrote her title.

She wrote a sentence.

She fixed the sentence.
She wrote another sentence,
and another, and another.
She did not stop to play with
Mr. Fuzz Dog.

She did not stop to sharpen her pencils.
She did not stop to call Lavender.

She wrote one sentence after the
other until she finished her paper.

The next day Mrs. Rose rang the Ringy Thing. "Class, your papers give some excellent instructions. Here is one of my favorites."

Poppy did not smooth her fur. She did not lick her paw. She did not polish her ear.

She sat very still.

How to Get in Trouble

by Poppy J. Thistleberry

To Get in Trouble is very simple.

First, talk in class even after you are told to be quiet. Then, be mean to someone who did better than you.

And try to copy that person's paper.

At home, call your brother Scraggle Tail.

Throw your notebook across the room.

At dinner, mush your food and spill your milk and say you don't care.

Stomp your feet and cry.

Last and worst of all, be rude to your very best friend and do not apologize.

This is my advice on How to Get in Trouble.

Follow these instructions and you can get in trouble, too.   The End.

The class clapped.
Poppy blushed and gave Lavender a shy look.
Lavender gave Poppy a big grin.

Poppy smoothed her fur. She licked her paw and polished her ear, and beamed a verrryyy huge smile.

For David, with gratitude for providing fertile soil,
and in memory of his mother—S. E.

For Mom, Poppy's number one fan—R. B.

Text copyright © 2015 by Susan Eaddy
Illustrations copyright © 2015 by Rosalinde Bonnet

Published by Charlesbridge, 85 Main Street, Watertown, MA 02472 • (617) 926-0329 • www.charlesbridge.com

Library of Congress Cataloging-in-Publication Data
Eaddy, Susan, author.
  Poppy's best paper / Susan Eaddy; illustrated by Rosalinde Bonnet.
    pages cm
  Summary: Poppy J. Thistleberry decides she wants to be a writer, but she is struggling to come up with material for her class writing assignments—and annoyed that her best friend, Lavender, keeps getting picked to read her paper.
    ISBN 978-1-58089-614-6 (reinforced for library use)
    ISBN 978-1-60734-911-2 (ebook)
    ISBN 978-1-60734-912-9 (ebook pdf)
1. Creative writing—Juvenile fiction. 2. Elementary schools—Juvenile fiction. 3. Best friends—Juvenile fiction. [1. Creative writing—Fiction. 2. Schools—Fiction. 3. Best friends—Fiction. 4. Friendship—Fiction. 5. Animals—Fiction.] I. Bonnet, Rosalinde, illustrator. II. Title.

PZ7.E1117Po 2015
813.54—dc23   2014010498

Printed in China
(hc) 10 9 8 7 6 5 4 3 2 1

Illustrations made with India ink, printing, watercolor, collage, and pencil on Arches watercolor cold-pressed 140-lb. paper
Text type set in Adobe Caslon and FG Noel
Color separations by Colourscan Print Co Pte Ltd, Singapore
Printed by 1010 Printing International Limited in Huizhou, Guangdong, China
Production supervision by Brian G. Walker
Designed by Susan Mallory Sherman